W9-ADL-175

01/2018

PALM BEACH COUNTY
LIBRARY SYSTEM
3650 Summit Boulevard
West Palm Beach, FL 33406-4198

Dear Parent:
Your child's love of reading starts here!

Every child learns to read in a different way and at his or her own speed. Some go back and forth between reading levels and read favorite books again and again. Others read through each level in order. You can help your young reader improve and become more confident by encouraging his or her own interests and abilities. From books your child reads with you to the first books he or she reads alone, there are I Can Read Books for every stage of reading:

SHARED READING
Basic language, word repetition, and whimsical illustrations, ideal for sharing with your emergent reader

BEGINNING READING
Short sentences, familiar words, and simple concepts for children eager to read on their own

READING WITH HELP
Engaging stories, longer sentences, and language play for developing readers

READING ALONE
Complex plots, challenging vocabulary, and high-interest topics for the independent reader

ADVANCED READING
Short paragraphs, chapters, and exciting themes for the perfect bridge to chapter books

I Can Read Books have introduced children to the joy of reading since 1957. Featuring award-winning authors and illustrators and a fabulous cast of beloved characters, I Can Read Books set the standard for beginning readers.

A lifetime of discovery begins with the magical words **"I Can Read!"**

*Visit www.icanread.com for information
on enriching your child's reading experience.*

For Brielle.
Have fun along the way.
—R.S.

I Can Read Book® is a trademark of HarperCollins Publishers.

Splat the Cat: The Name of the Game
Copyright © 2012 by Rob Scotton
All rights reserved. Printed in the United States of America.
No part of this book may be used or reproduced in any manner whatsoever without written permission except in the case of brief quotations embodied in critical articles and reviews. For information address HarperCollins Children's Books, a division of HarperCollins Publishers, 195 Broadway, New York, NY 10007.
www.icanread.com
Library of Congress catalog card number: 2011941960
ISBN 978-0-06-209015-7 (trade bdg.) —ISBN 978-0-06-209014-0 (pbk.)

14 15 16 17 18 LP/WOR 10 9 8 7 6 5 4 3   ❖   First Edition

I Can Read!

BEGINNING 1 READING

Splat the Cat
The Name of the Game

Based on the bestselling books by Rob Scotton

Cover art by Rob Scotton

Text by Amy Hsu Lin

Interior illustrations by Robert Eberz

HARPER

An Imprint of HarperCollins Publishers

Spike and Plank were

at Splat's house to play games.

"Let's play Mouse, Mouse, Cat,"
said Splat.

"I'll go first," Spike said.

"Mouse . . . mouse . . . cat!" he said.

Spike tagged Splat.

Splat tripped

when he chased Spike.

SPLAT!

"What a shame,"

said Splat's little sister.

"So sad, too bad.

You lost the game!"

"Let's play hide-and-seek!

I'll be it," said Plank.

Splat said, "Don't peek!"

Plank began to count.

Spike went to hide.

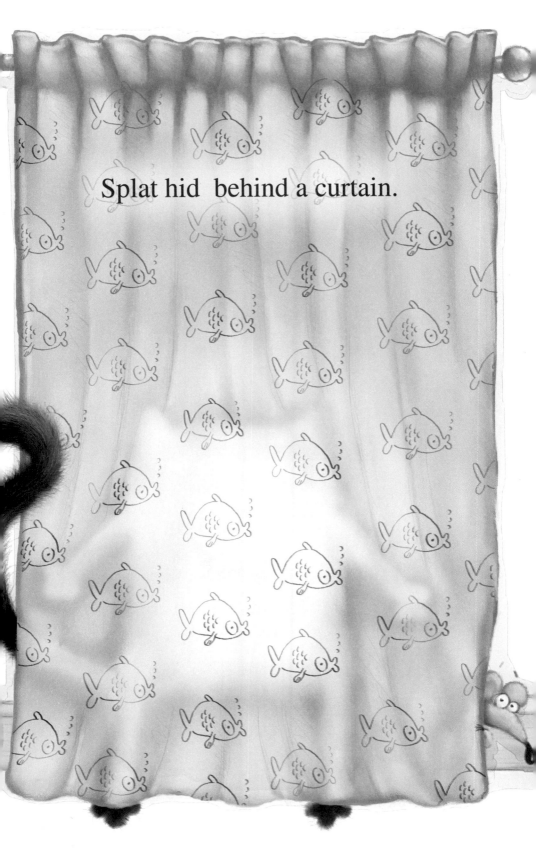

Splat hid behind a curtain.

Plank found Splat right away.

"That spot was tame.

So sad, too bad.

You lost the game!"

said Little Sis.

No one could find Spike.

"Good spot, Spike!" said Plank.

"You win!" said Splat.

"I want to play," said Little Sis.

"Fine. You're it," said Splat.

Splat, Spike, and Plank went to hide.

This time Splat found a great spot:

a sooty fireplace with no flame.

Splat's nose itched.

"ACHOO!"

Little Sis
found him right away.
"That's lame," she said.
"So sad, too bad.
You lost the game!"

Little Sis found

Spike and Plank, too.

"Yippee! I win," she said.

"I get all the fame."

"Why don't I ever win?" Splat said.

"You almost did," said Spike.

"Maybe the next game," said Plank.

"So sad, too bad.
You lost the game!"
said Little Sis.

Splat shook his head.

"No more games," he said.

"But that's why we came,"

said Spike.

"How about Go Fish?" Plank said.

"Or Freeze Cat?" Spike said.

"Or jump rope?" said Little Sis.

"You can play without me," said Splat.

Splat started to play by himself.

Spike, Plank, and Little Sis

played together, too.

Playing alone was not much fun.

"Now this is a shame.

It's tame and lame!" said Splat.

"This isn't the same," said Spike.

"Not without Splat," said Plank.

"No, it isn't," said Little Sis.

"What are you playing?

And can I play, too?" asked Splat.

"Any game you like," said Plank.

"Play with us again!" said Spike.

"Please, Splat?" asked Little Sis.

"Okay," Splat said with a smile.

"Let's play hide-and-seek

just one more time."

"I'll be it," said Spike.

He began to count.

This time, Splat thought of

the best place of all to hide.

27

Spike found Plank first.

Then he found Little Sis.

Then the friends looked for Splat,

but they couldn't find him.

Plank said, "Splat, come out!"

Spike said, "Splat, where are you?"

Little Sis said, "Come out,
come out, wherever you are."

"Here I am!

I'm in the frame!" said Splat.

"You win!" said Spike.

"You win!" said Plank.

"You won the game!" said Little Sis.

"I win because I have
the best friends," said Splat.